"Well, I'm very glad you're home, Bear. Next time you want to go camping, give me a ring. I'll come along. I'll always be by your side, Bear. Always and forever."

"Always and forever? Sigh."

"Did you make any friends?"

"No."

"Did you catch any fish?"

"You already said that."

"So, before I found you . . . did you catch any fish at all, Bear?"

"No."

"Did you enjoy the rain?"

"No."

"Did you have fun?"

"No."

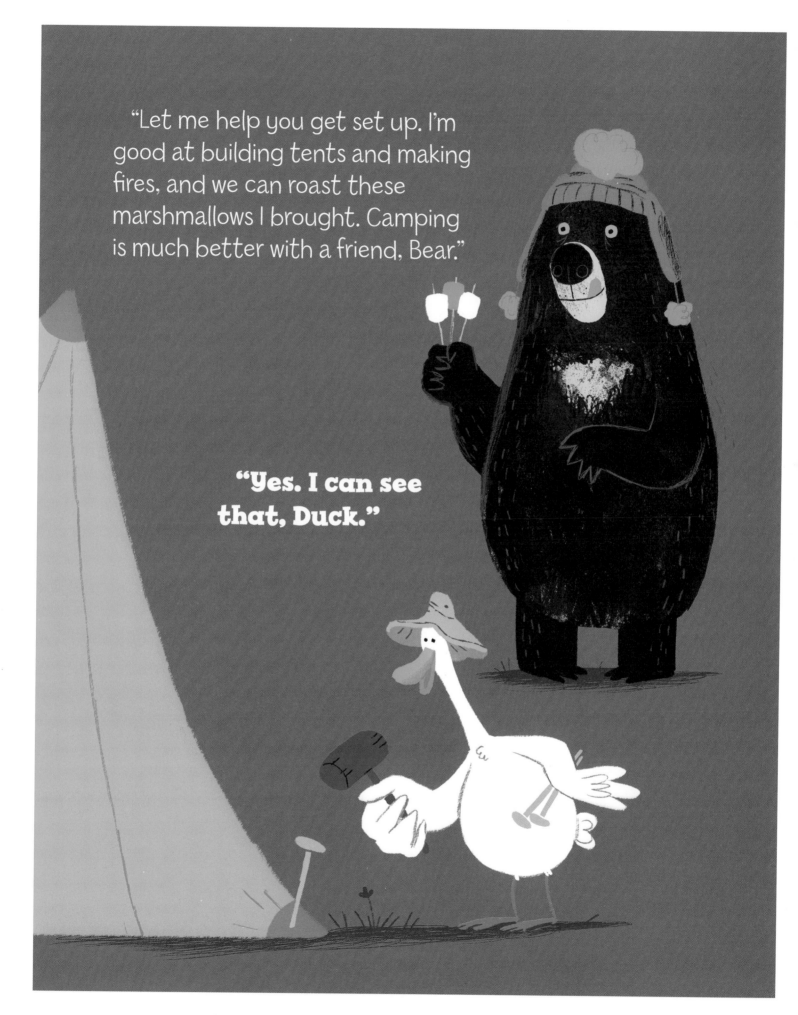

"Let me help you get set up. I'm good at building tents and making fires, and we can roast these marshmallows I brought. Camping is much better with a friend, Bear."

"Yes. I can see that, Duck."

"Duck, I'm actually SO relieved to see you!"

"You are?"

"Absolutely! Please stay. Keep me company. We can go back home together in the morning."

"That sounds wonderful, Bear! Perfect. Sublime. I actually thought you wanted to get away from me."

"Bear! It's me. Duck! From next door. I found you, ol' buddy, ol' pal, ol' chum. Are you hungry? Are you cold?
Are you scared?
Why were you screaming?
Why was I screaming?"

"Duck? Duck? Is it really you? How did you find me?"

"I wanted you to come home, so I tracked you through the woods. I missed you. Come home already, Bear!"

"Nothing to worry about here.
Nothing to worry about at all. . . ."

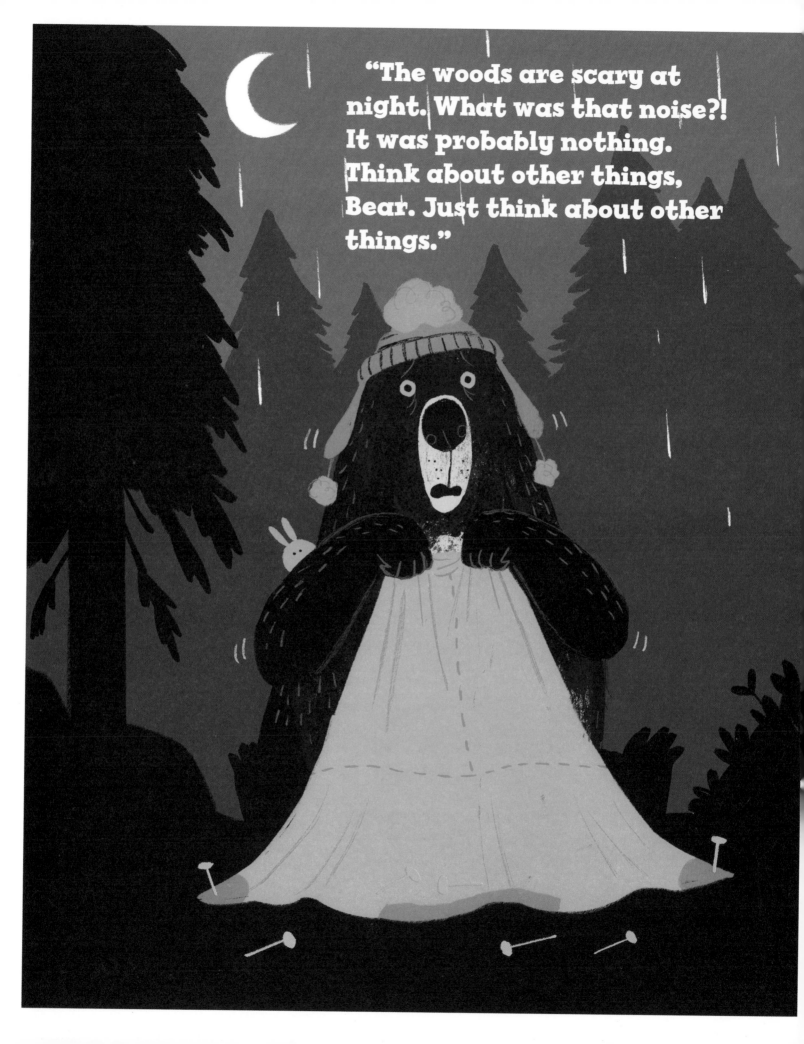

"The woods are scary at night. What was that noise?! It was probably nothing. Think about other things, Bear. Just think about other things."

"There's really only one thing to do. I have to catch up with Bear. He'll surely need my help. After all, I know how to catch fish with my beak.

Also, I'm great company!

Fishing can be really lonely.

Plus it's raining."

"Gotta find Bear, gotta find Bear,
it's getting dark, gotta find Bear . . ."

"I haven't caught a single fish. And I forgot to bring snacks. I miss my refrigerator."

"I'm drenched. I'm hungry. I don't know how to start a campfire. And I'm just so tired."

"Ugh. There's got to be an easier way to set up a tent. Ah, never mind. I'll figure it out later. Time for some fishing."

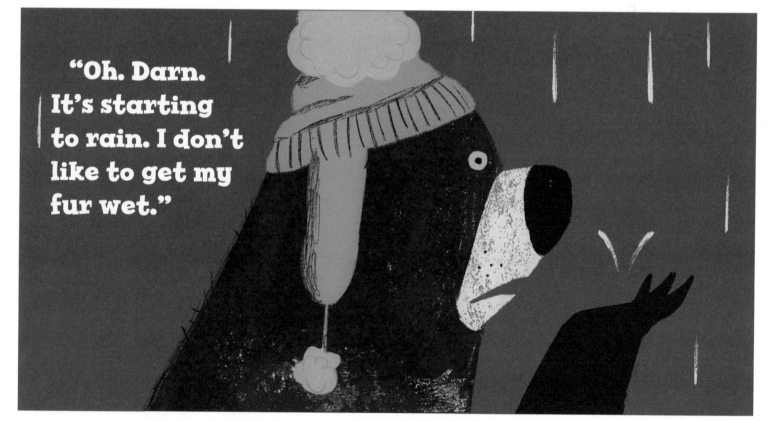

"Oh. Darn. It's starting to rain. I don't like to get my fur wet."

"COME HOME ALREADY, BEAR!"

"I'm just so bored! I wonder what ol' Bear is doing right this second. I bet he's having so much fun without me."

"Sigh. I really don't feel like doing any of these things. I miss my friend."

So Bear left without me and I'm all alone.

I'll be fine! Ha ha! Yes!
Ha!
Ha!
Ha!
I'm just fine!

After all, I can entertain myself!"

"Ah, yes. This is the life. Alone with my thoughts. No pesky neighbors knocking on my door at all hours. It's nice to be by myself for once. Ahhhhhhhhhhhhh."

FISHING?!

What am I going to do with myself until then?!"

"Bear's gone fishing?
He's back next week?

BEAR'S GONE FISHING?
HE'S BACK NEXT WEEK?

He's gone fishing?
Without me?
But ...
but ...

NEXT WEEK?!

"Wait a minute...."

"Get ready for some more fun times, Bear!"

KNOCK KNOCK

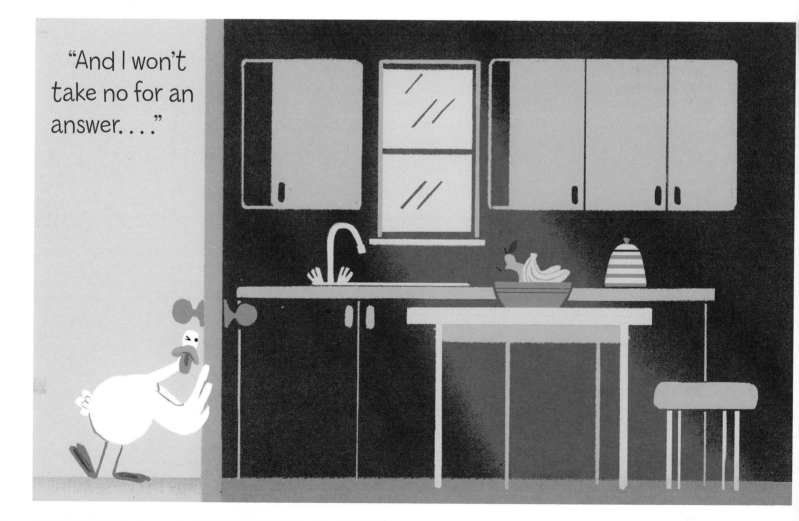

"And I won't take no for an answer. . . ."

"I wonder what ol' Bear is up to. . . ."

"Another glorious morning full of possibility!"

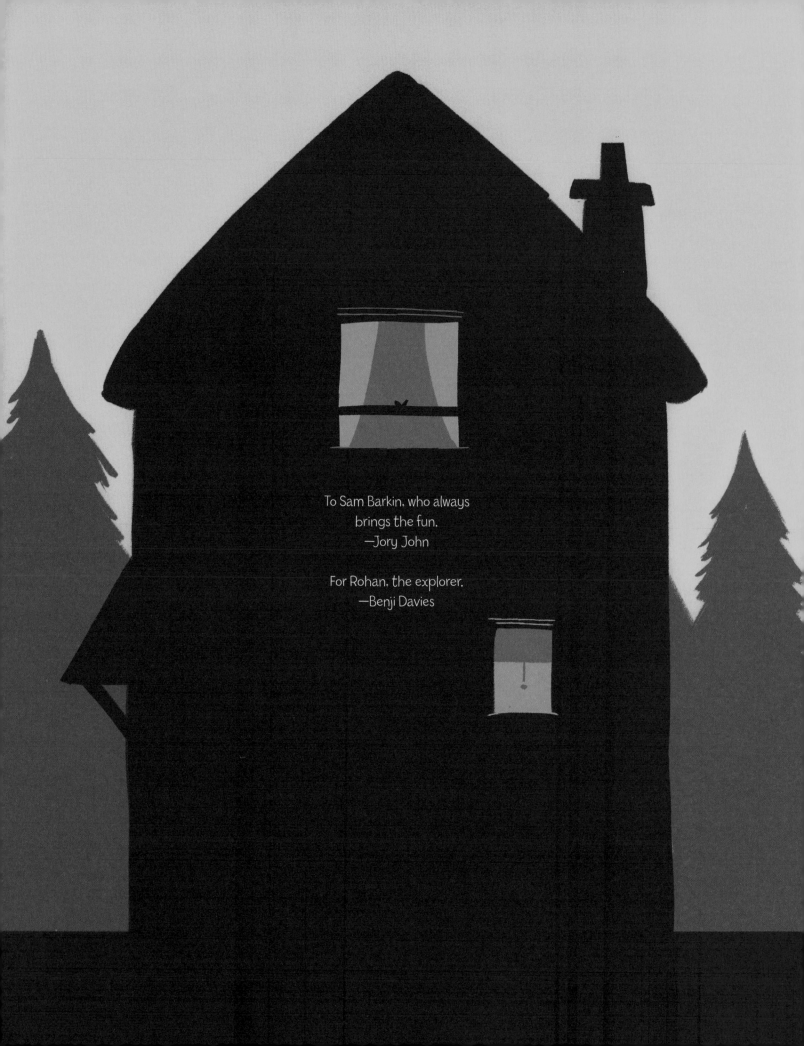

To Sam Barkin, who always
brings the fun.
—Jory John

For Rohan, the explorer.
—Benji Davies